The Tale of Jemima Puddle-Duck

by
Beatrix Potter™

Grange
BOOKS

WHAT a funny sight it is to see a brood of ducklings with a hen!

—Listen to the story of Jemima Puddle-duck, who was annoyed because the farmer's wife would not let her hatch her own eggs.

Her sister-in-law, Mrs. Rebeccah Puddle-duck, was perfectly willing to leave the hatching to some one else.

"I HAVE not the patience to sit on a nest for twenty-eight days; and no more have you, Jemima. You would let them go cold; you know you would!"

"I wish to hatch them all by myself," quacked Jemima Puddle-duck. She tried to hide her eggs; but they were always found and carried off.

Jemima Puddle-duck became quite desperate. She determined to make a nest right away from the farm.

S HE set off on a fine spring afternoon along the cart-road that leads over the hill.

She was wearing a shawl and a poke bonnet.

When she reached the top of the hill, she saw a wood in the distance. She thought that it looked a safe quiet spot.

Jemima Puddle-duck was not much in the habit of flying.

SHE ran downhill a few yards flapping her shawl, and then she jumped off into the air.

She flew beautifully when she had got a good start.

She skimmed along over the tree-tops until she saw an open place in the middle of the wood, where the trees and brush-wood had been cleared.

Jemima alighted rather heavily, and began to waddle about in search of a convenient dry nesting-place. She rather fancied a tree-stump amongst some tall fox-gloves.

B UT—seated upon the stump, she was startled to find an elegantly dressed gentleman reading a newspaper.

He had black prick ears and sandy coloured whiskers.

"Quack?" said Jemima Puddle-duck, with her head and her bonnet on one side—"Quack?"

THE gentleman raised his eyes above his newspaper and looked curiously at Jemima—

"Madam, have you lost your way?" said he. He had a long bushy tail which he was sitting upon, as the stump was somewhat damp.

Jemima thought him mighty civil and handsome. She explained that she had not lost her way, but that she was trying to find a convenient dry nesting-place.

"Ah? is that so? indeed!" said the gentleman with sandy whiskers, looking curiously at Jemima. He folded up the newspaper, and put it in his coat-tail pocket.

JEMIMA complained of the superfluous hen.

"Indeed? how interesting? I wish I could meet with that fowl. I would teach it to mind its own business!"

"But as to a nest—there is no difficulty: I have a sackful of feathers in my wood-shed. No, my dear madam, you will be in nobody's way. You may sit there as long as you like," said the bushy long-tailed gentleman.

HE led the way to a very retired, dismal-looking house amongst the fox-gloves.

It was built of faggots and turf, and there were two broken pails, one on top of another, by way of a chimney.

"This is my summer residence; you would not find my earth—my winter house—so convenient," said the hospitable gentleman.

THERE was a tumble-down shed at the back of the house, made of old soap-boxes. The gentleman opened the door, and showed Jemima in.

The shed was almost quite full of feathers—it was almost suffocating; but it was comfortable and very soft.

JEMIMA PUDDLE-DUCK was rather surprised to find
such a vast quantity of feathers. But it was very comfortable;
and she made a nest without any trouble at all.

When she came out, the sandy whiskered gentleman was
sitting on a log reading the newspaper—at least he had it
spread out, but he was looking over the top of it.

H E was so polite, that he seemed almost sorry to let
Jemima go home for the night. He promised to take
great care of her nest until she came back again next day.

He said he loved eggs and ducklings; he should be proud to
see a fine nestful in his wood-shed.

Jemima Puddle-duck came every afternoon; she laid nine
eggs in the nest. They were greeny white and very large. The
foxy gentleman admired them immensely. He used to turn
them over and count them when Jemima was not there.

AT last Jemima told him that she intended to begin to sit next day—"and I will bring a bag of corn with me, so that I need never leave my nest until the eggs are hatched. They might catch cold," said the conscientious Jemima.

"Madam, I beg you not to trouble yourself with a bag; I will provide oats. But before you commence your tedious sitting, I intend to give you a treat. Let us have a dinner-party all to ourselves!

"MAY I ask you to bring up some herbs from the farm-garden to make a savoury omelette? Sage and thyme, and mint and two onions, and some parsley. I will provide lard for the stuff—lard for the omelette," said the hospitable gentleman with sandy whiskers.

Jemima Puddle-duck was a simpleton: not even the mention of sage and onions made her suspicious.

She went round the farm-garden, nibbling off snippets of all the different sorts of herbs that are used for stuffing roast duck.

And she waddled into the kitchen, and got two onions out of a basket.

14

THE collie-dog Kep met her coming out, "What are you doing with those onions? Where do you go every afternoon by yourself, Jemima Puddle-duck?"

Jemima was rather in awe of the collie; she told him the whole story.

The collie listened, with his wise head on one side; he grinned when she described the polite gentleman with sandy whiskers.

He asked several questions about the wood, and about the exact position of the house and shed.

THEN he went out, and trotted down the village.

He went to look for two fox-hound puppies who were out at walk with the butcher.

Jemima Puddle-duck went up the cart-road for the last time, on a sunny afternoon. She was rather burdened with bunches of herbs and two onions in a bag.

SHE flew over the wood, and alighted opposite the house of the bushy long-tailed gentleman.

He was sitting on a log; he sniffed the air, and kept glancing uneasily round the wood. When Jemima alighted he quite jumped.

"Come into the house as soon as you have looked at your eggs. Give me the herbs for the omelette. Be sharp!"

HE was rather abrupt. Jemima Puddle-duck had never heard him speak like that.

She felt surprised, and uncomfortable.

While she was inside she heard pattering feet round the back of the shed. Some one with a black nose sniffed at the bottom of the door, and then locked it.

Jemima became much alarmed.

A moment afterwards there were most awful noises—barking, baying, growls and howls, squealing and groans.

AND nothing more was ever seen of that foxy-whiskered
gentleman.

Presently Kep opened the door of the shed, and let out
Jemima Puddle-duck.

Unfortunately the puppies rushed in and gobbled up all the
eggs before he could stop them.

He had a bite on his ear and both the puppies were limping.

19

JEMIMA PUDDLE-DUCK was escorted home in tears on account of those eggs.

She laid some more in June, and she was permitted to keep them herself: but only four of them hatched.

Jemima Puddle-duck said that it was because of her nerves; but she had always been a bad sitter.

THE END

VOLUME 8
DARKSEID
WAR
PART 2

JUSTICE LEAGUE

JUSTICE LEAGUE

VOLUME 8
DARKSEID WAR PART 2

WRITTEN BY
GEOFF JOHNS

ART BY
JASON FABOK
FRANCIS MANAPUL
IVAN REIS
JOE PRADO
OSCAR JIMENEZ
PAUL PELLETIER
TONY KORDOS

COLOR BY
BRAD ANDERSON
FRANCIS MANAPUL
ALEX SINCLAIR
BRIAN BUCCELLATO

LETTERS BY
ROB LEIGH

COLLECTION COVER ART BY
JASON FABOK
& BRAD ANDERSON

SUPERMAN CREATED BY
JERRY SIEGEL &
JOE SHUSTER
BY SPECIAL ARRANGEMENT
WITH THE JERRY SIEGEL FAMILY

THE FOURTH WORLD CREATED BY
JACK KIRBY

BRIAN CUNNINGHAM Editor – Original Series
AMEDEO TURTURRO Assistant Editor – Original Series
JEB WOODARD Group Editor – Collected Editions
ROBIN WILDMAN Editor – Collected Edition
STEVE COOK Design Director – Books
DAMIAN RYLAND Publication Design

BOB HARRAS Senior VP – Editor-in-Chief, DC Comics

DIANE NELSON President
DAN DIDIO and JIM LEE Co-Publishers
GEOFF JOHNS Chief Creative Officer
AMIT DESAI Senior VP – Marketing & Global Franchise Management
NAIRI GARDINER Senior VP – Finance
SAM ADES VP – Digital Marketing
BOBBIE CHASE VP – Talent Development
MARK CHIARELLO Senior VP – Art, Design & Collected Editions
JOHN CUNNINGHAM VP – Content Strategy
ANNE DEPIES VP – Strategy Planning & Reporting
DON FALLETTI VP – Manufacturing Operations
LAWRENCE GANEM VP – Editorial Administration & Talent Relations
ALISON GILL Senior VP – Manufacturing & Operations
HANK KANALZ Senior VP – Editorial Strategy & Administration
JAY KOGAN VP – Legal Affairs
DEREK MADDALENA Senior VP – Sales & Business Development
JACK MAHAN VP – Business Affairs
DAN MIRON VP – Sales Planning & Trade Development
NICK NAPOLITANO VP – Manufacturing Administration
CAROL ROEDER VP – Marketing
EDDIE SCANNELL VP – Mass Account & Digital Sales
COURTNEY SIMMONS Senior VP – Publicity & Communications
JIM (SKI) SOKOLOWSKI VP – Comic Book Specialty & Newsstand Sales
SANDY YI Senior VP – Global Franchise Management

JUSTICE LEAGUE VOLUME 8: DARKSEID WAR PART 2

DC Comics, 2900 West Alameda Ave., Burbank, CA 91505
Printed by RR Donnelley, Salem, VA, USA. 8/19/16. First Printing.
ISBN: 978-1-4012-6341-6

Library of Congress Cataloging-in-Publication Data is available.

GEOFF JOHNS writer **FRANCIS MANAPUL** artist **FRANCIS MANAPUL WITH BRIAN BUCCELLATO** colorists **ROB LEIGH** letterer

AMEDEO TURTURRO assistant editor **BRIAN CUNNINGHAM** group editor cover by **FRANCIS MANAPUL**

DARKSEID

IS

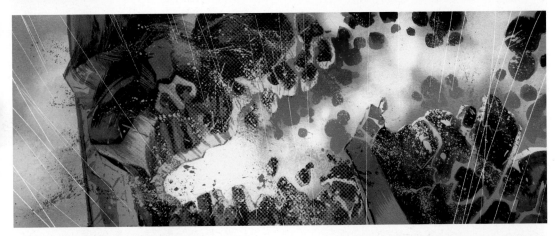

DEAD.

SINCE THE DAY HUMANS LOOKED UP TO GODS, THEY HAVE WONDERED...

NEW GODS ARE BORN.

DID I KILL DARKSEID?

YOU DIDN'T KILL HIM, FLASH.

IT WAS SO AWFUL. I COULD FEEL HIM DIE. I COULD SEE IT.

THE BLACK RACER DID IT, NOT YOU.

WHAT OR WHO IS THE BLACK RACER?

DARKSEID'S GREATEST WEAPON. HE CLAIMED HE'D *CAPTURED* DEATH, OR AN *ASPECT* OF IT, WHEN HE FIRST TOOK CONTROL OF APOKOLIPS.

BUT DEATH COULD ONLY BE COMMUNICATED WITH BY ANCHORING IT TO A *SENTIENT HOST.*

DARKSEID MAY HAVE SUMMONED THE RACER, BUT SOMEHOW THE ANTI-MONITOR TOOK CONTROL OF IT. FORCED *YOU* TO BOND WITH IT, FLASH.

I'M SORRY.

WHY ARE YOU APOLOGIZING, MISTER MIRACLE?

BECAUSE NOT EVEN I COULD ESCAPE BEING *FUSED* WITH THE RACER. ONCE A HOST IS CHOSEN, THEY'RE BOUND UNTIL THEY--

I'M NOT LIKE THE OTHER HOSTS. AND I DON'T WANT TO ESCAPE DEATH.

I WANT TO *CONTROL* IT.

THE FLASH
GOD OF DEATH

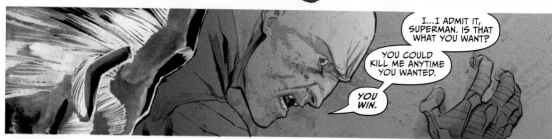

SUPERMAN
GOD OF STRENGTH

BATMAN
GOD OF
KNOWLEDGE

WHY ARE YOU *BOWING* BEFORE HIM?

HE HASN'T *EARNED* IT YET.

"I'M *DEATH*."

WE SHOULD ALL BE CONCERNED BY THAT, RIGHT? I'M NOT NEARLY AS FAST AS FLASH, BUT I BET CYBORG CAN TRACK--

AAAHH!

I will *not* give my power to *this* boy, wizard!

HE WILL BE MY VESSEL.

HE WILL BURN, LIKE ALL MARTIANS.

THE SOURCE WALL WILL NOT STAND FOR LONG.

BILLY? BILLY, LISTEN TO ME!

**SHAZAM
GOD OF GODS**

THE NEW GODS CALL YOU!

KRAKKOOOM

I HEARD VOICES COMING FROM HIM.

I HEAR *VOICES.* DID YOU--

WE NEED TO SPLIT UP. SOME OF US GO AFTER SHAZAM. THE OTHERS AFTER FLASH.

DARKSEID'S DEAD. THAT'S SUPPOSED TO BE A *GOOD THING.* BUT WHAT DID HIS DEATH ACTUALLY *MEAN?*

WHAT THE HELL IS GOING ON WITH EVERYONE?

I WOULDN'T WORRY ABOUT THEM.

WAKE UP, HUMAN.

...WHAT?

YOU HAVE CLAIMED TO BE THIS HERO. THE CHOSEN ONE TO LEAD APOKOLIPS TO A NEW AGE.

WITH DARKSEID'S DEATH, HIS *OMEGA EFFECT* HAS BEEN UNLEASHED.

IT WILL RETURN HERE TO APOKOLIPS.

WE WILL *CONTAIN* IT.

IN *YOU.*

WAIT--

IF YOU ARE A HERO *WORTHY* OF THIS POWER AS YOU CLAIM, YOU WILL SURVIVE.

PING

IF NOT, YOU WILL DIE.

I SEE A *RED STAR!*

ARDORA!

NOT A RED STAR. THE *OMEGA EFFECT.* IT RETURNS.

THE TEST IS NOW, HUMAN.

"GRAIL?"

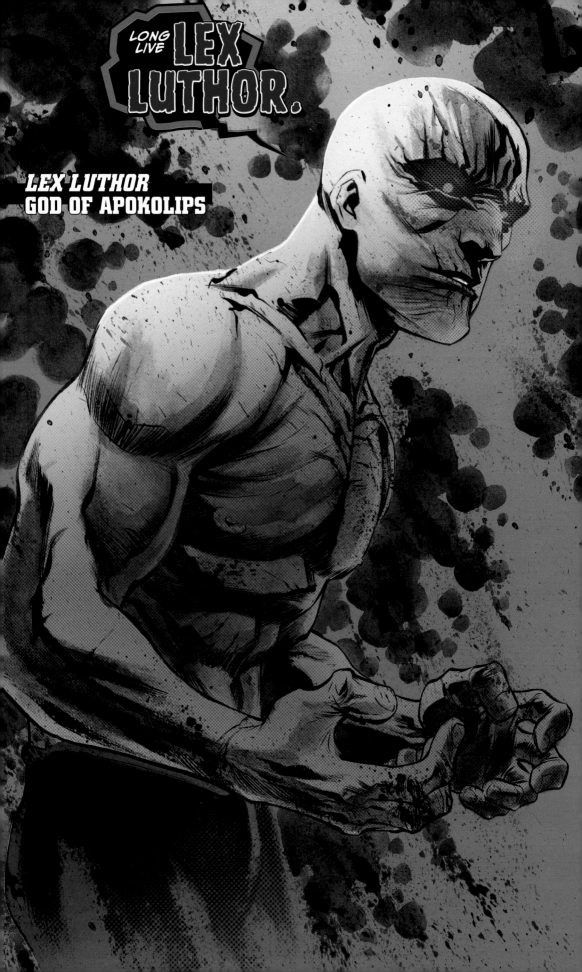

DARKSEID WAR CHAPTER SIX: AFTER DEATH PART TWO

GEOFF JOHNS writer **FRANCIS MANAPUL** artist **FRANCIS MANAPUL** colorist **ROB LEIGH** letterer **AMEDEO TURTURRO** assistant editor **BRIAN CUNNINGHAM** group editor
cover by **FRANCIS MANAPUL**

GODS AREN'T ALWAYS BORN.

SOMETIMES THEY'RE MADE.

BATMAN
GOD OF KNOWLEDGE

RAW CLAY GIVEN PURPOSE. SCULPTED BY DESTINY. TOUCHED BY THE DIVINE.

SUPERMAN
GOD OF STRENGTH

OR SO GO THE TALES SOME CHILDREN ARE TOLD.

THERE'S ANOTHER TALE ABOUT A WOMAN. SHE WAS NAMED QUEEN INO OF THEBES. ONE NIGHT, DURING A MYSTERIOUS LIGHTNING STORM, INO'S SISTER GAVE BIRTH TO A SON.

BUT SHE WAS UNABLE TO RAISE THE BABY--SO INO TOOK THE BOY IN AS HER OWN.

THE FLASH
GOD OF DEATH

WHAT INO DIDN'T KNOW WAS THAT THIS BABY WAS THE SON OF ZEUS--

--AND WHEN HERA LEARNED OF THE BOY'S EXISTENCE AND HER HUSBAND'S BETRAYAL, SHE WENT INTO A RAGE.

SHAZAM
GOD OF GODS

HERA TOOK REVENGE ON INO FOR RAISING THE BOY. FIRST, SHE DROVE INO'S HUSBAND MAD ENOUGH THAT HE TOOK HIS OWN LIFE--

--THEN HERA STRUCK INO WITH THAT SAME MADNESS.

GREEN LANTERN
GOD OF LIGHT

BLINDED BY HERA'S INFECTION, INO BOILED HER OWN SON IN A CAULDRON.

WHEN HER SANITY RETURNED, INO WAS SO HORRIFIED BY WHAT SHE HAD DONE SHE TOOK THE BODY OF HER SON AND LEAPT OFF THE CLIFFS AND INTO THE SEA.

INO SHOULD HAVE DIED.

BUT SHE DIDN'T.

LEX LUTHOR
GOD OF APOKOLIPS

WHERE IS HE, AMAZON?!

WHERE IS THE ANTI-MONITOR?!

YOU LOOK LIKE A GREEN LANTERN.

I'VE SLAYED PLENTY OF GREEN LANTERNS.

I'M NOT A GREEN LANTERN.

YOU'RE ANNOYING, IS WHAT YOU ARE, VOLTHOOM.

AND YOU ARE PATHETIC, JESSICA. WIELDING THE RING LIKE A FRIGHTENED CHILD.

ONLY I CAN USE THIS RING PROPERLY. MY WILL--

L-LET GO--

NO.

IF I DO NOTHING, YOU'LL KILL US BOTH!

AAAHHH!

LET THEM *TRY* AND DO SOMETHING ABOUT IT.

WE WILL, BARDA.

DARKSEID MAY BE DEAD, BUT WE LIVE ON. FOR HIM. FOR DARKSEID.

WHY? IF THE GREAT DARKNESS IS DEAD, LET IT ALL FINALLY BE OVER, LASHINA. AT LEAST BETWEEN US.

TELL GRANNY AND THE OTHER FURIES THAT. I PROPOSE A CLEAN SLATE HERE AND NOW. YOU LEAVE SCOT AND I BE AND WE'LL DO THE SAME TO YOU.

YOUR BETRAYAL WILL NEVER BE FORGOTTEN, BARDA. YOU'VE BROKEN THE BLACK OATH OF THE FURIES.

WE WILL NEVER STOP.

YOU WILL IF I GET AHOLD OF YOU.

BAH!! IT IS NOT THEM THAT I SEEK TO TEAR APART NOW.

WE WILL FIND THE ANTI-MONITOR OURSELVES! FOR KALIBAK!

AND FOR MY FATHER.

FOR DARKSEID.

WITHOUT THE *MOBIUS CHAIR*, YOU'RE LOST, METRON.

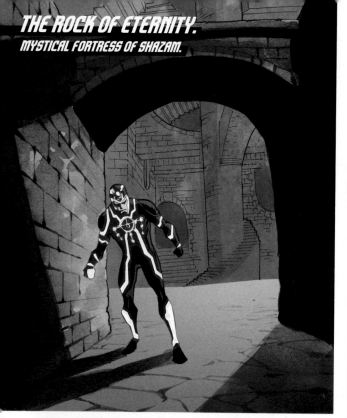

WHO ARE YOU?

A FRIEND OF BILLY BATSON'S, BUT NOT OF YOURS, I SUSPECT. WHAT ARE YOU UP TO, METRON? WHAT ARE YOU DOING?

IF IT'S WHAT I BELIEVE, YOU'VE TRADED THE SAFETY OF THE UNIVERSE FOR YOUR OWN SOUL. IF MOBIUS RETURNS TO HIS CHAIR--

QUIET.

I WANT QUIET.

WHAT ARE THESE *SHADOW SOLDIERS* DOING, GRAIL?

THE SHADOW DEMONS ARE TRYING TO PROTECT THE ANTI-MONITOR FROM US. YET WE WERE HIS ALLIES. WITH DARKSEID DEAD, THEY SHOULD HAVE DISPERSED.

WHAT IS *THE ANTI-MONITOR* DOING?

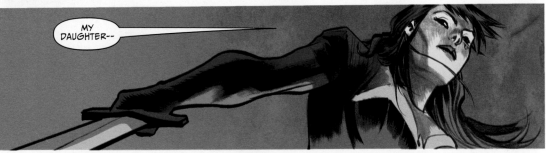

MY DAUGHTER--

PATIENCE, MOTHER. THIS IS NOT OVER. NOT YET.

ULTRAMAN.
SUPERWOMAN.
OWLMAN.

THEY CALLED THEMSELVES
THE CRIME SYNDICATE.

THEY CAME FROM
A PARALLEL WORLD.
ONE THAT WAS DESTROYED
BY THE ANTI-MONITOR.

THEY TRIED TO TAKE
OVER OURS. AND I'LL
ADMIT THAT IF IT WASN'T
FOR LEX LUTHOR, THEY
MAY HAVE SUCCEEDED.

THE CRIME
SYNDICATE FOUGHT
THE ANTI-MONITOR.

THEY KNOW HIM
BETTER THAN WE DO.

THEY COULD KNOW
WHY HE'S HERE.

OR HOW TO *STOP* HIM.

WE MIGHT BE ABLE TO GET THE ANSWERS FROM THE REMAINING MEMBERS OF THE SYNDICATE.

BATMAN AND GREEN LANTERN WERE SUPPOSED TO DO RECON ON THE ANTI-MONITOR--

BATMAN'S NOT RESPONDING TO MY CALLS, JESSICA. AND I'M GETTING SOME KIND OF *FEEDBACK* WHENEVER I TRY AND CONNECT TO LANTERN'S RING.

OWLMAN'S BEEN MISSING SINCE THE SYNDICATE WAS TAKEN APART, BUT ULTRAMAN AND SUPERWOMAN ARE BEING HELD IN BELLE REVE.

HATE TO MAKE THINGS MORE COMPLICATED THAN THEY ARE, BUT A.R.G.U.S. CLASSIFIED ULTRAMAN AND SUPERWOMAN AS LEVEL ZERO INMATES.

WHICH MEANS NO ONE GETS IN TO SEE THEM. INCLUDING THE LEAGUE.

YOU WANT TO *TALK* TO THE SYNDICATE, WE'LL HAVE TO BREAK INTO BELLE REVE TO DO IT.

WHATEVER A BELLE REVE IS, IT SOUNDS LIKE FUN.

YOU NEED TO GET IN SOMEWHERE--

--I CAN GET YOU IN.

LEARN WHAT YOU CAN. AND STAY TOGETHER.

I'LL FIND THE REST OF THE LEAGUE AND THEN WE'LL MAKE A PLAN TO LOCATE AND RESTRAIN THE ANTI-MONITOR.

DIANA?

AS LONG AS I'VE KNOWN YOU, I HAVEN'T SEEN YOU WORRY MUCH. YOU LOOK WORRIED, DI.

I AM, STEVE.

AN *AMAZON* STARTED THIS. AN AMAZON I'VE NEVER HEARD ANYONE SPEAK OF BEFORE. ONE WHO HAD *DARKSEID'S CHILD.* ONE WHO USED THAT CHILD TO *START* THIS WAR AND, WITH THE *DEATH* OF *DARKSEID*, RELEASE HERA KNOWS *WHAT* INTO THE WORLD.

THE LEAGUE IS SPLIT APART.

TURNED INTO GODS.

I DON'T WORRY OFTEN. AND I NEVER GET COLD.

TODAY I'M BOTH.

WHEREVER YOU'RE GOING NEXT, I'M COMING WITH YOU.

IT'S DANGEROUS.

WHEN ISN'T IT FOR US?

IS THAT WHY YOU CHOSE HIM?

WHO?

MISTER MIRACLE AND HIS WIFE HAVE SOME KIND OF HEIGHTENED ABILITIES. COLORFUL COSTUMES. AND THEY CLEARLY WORK TOGETHER ON THE BATTLEFIELD.

THEY'RE IN LOVE. THAT MUCH I CAN SEE.

SUPERMAN AND I AREN'T IN LOVE, STEVE.

THEN WHAT ARE YOU?

FRIENDS.

DON'T MAKE ME USE THE LASSO ON YOU--

MORE THAN FRIENDS. BUT I DON'T KNOW WHAT THAT MEANS. AND NOW'S NOT THE TIME TO--

DI...IF THIS IS THE END. I JUST WANT YOU TO KNOW. I STILL... I'LL ALWAYS...

I HEARD MY NAME.

"I'VE BEEN HUNTING IT MY WHOLE LIFE.

SEARCHING FOR MY *TOOL* OF *VENGEANCE.*

"SUFFERING THROUGH UNSPEAKABLE HORRORS.

"I SACRIFICED *EVERYTHING* TO THE *DARKNESS.*

"ALL FOR *THIS.*

"THEY WILL TRY AND STOP US, MOTHER.

BUT IT'S *TOO LATE.*

MOBIUS HAS *SEPARATED* FROM IT.

WHAT IS IT?

"IT'S THE MOST POWERFUL FORCE IN THE UNIVERSE, MOTHER.

IT'S OURS.

THE ANTI-LIFE EQUATION IS OURS.

"MY FATHER'S ULTIMATE WEAPON BELONGS TO US."

THE ANTI-LIFE EQUATION? THIS IS WHAT YOU WERE AFTER?

BUT WHY, DAUGHTER?

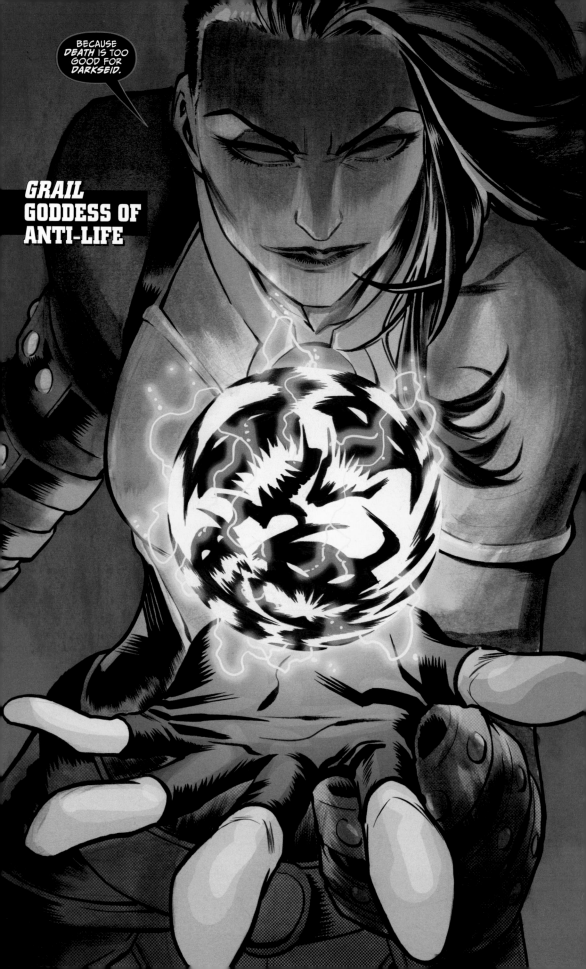

DARKSEID WAR CHAPTER SEVEN: GODS OF JUSTICE PART ONE
GEOFF JOHNS writer · **JASON FABOK** artist · **BRAD ANDERSON** colorist · **ROB LEIGH** letterer · **AMEDEO TURTURRO** assistant editor · **BRIAN CUNNINGHAM** group editor
cover by **JASON FABOK AND BRAD ANDERSON**

I'M NEVER LEAVING THIS CHAIR.

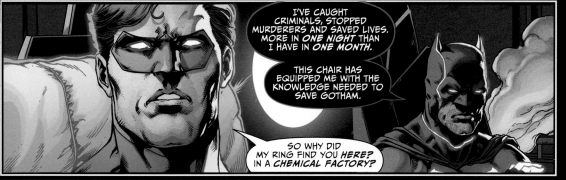

DARKSEID DIES AND MY FRIENDS UNDERGO A TRANSFORMATION.

BATMAN BECOMES A GOD OF KNOWLEDGE. FLASH, A GOD OF DEATH. NOW THIS.

DARKSEID'S DEMISE...IT'S LI AN EMPTINES: WAS CREATED AND THE UNIVER IS DESPERATE TO FILL IT.

I ONLY WANT TO SEE HOW STRONG YOU ARE.

THAT'S ALL.

HE'S NOT THINKING CLEARLY.

ARGGHHH!

I'VE GOT TO--

GOOD.

FIGHT ME.

"WE'RE THE *JUSTICE LEAGUE.* WHY CAN'T WE WALK UP TO THE *FRONT DOOR?*"

STEVE TREVOR SAID *ULTRAMAN* AND *SUPERWOMAN* WERE RECLASSIFIED AS LEVEL ZERO INMATES BY *A.R.G.U.S.--* MEANING *NO ONE* GETS IN TO SEE THEM.

I'VE LOOPED THE SECURITY CAMERAS, SCOT. NOW I'M SHUTTING OFF THE PERIMETER ALARMS.

I ALREADY SHUT THEM OFF, CYBORG.

THEN I'LL DISABLE THE MOTION SENSORS UP AHEAD--

ALREADY DID IT.

DON'T TELL ME YOU'VE ALREADY DIVERTED THE GUARDS, TOO?

NO.

MY WIFE'S DOING THAT.

"IT'S WHAT HE LIVES FOR."

ELSEWHERE.

 WHAT ARE YOU DOING, GRAIL?

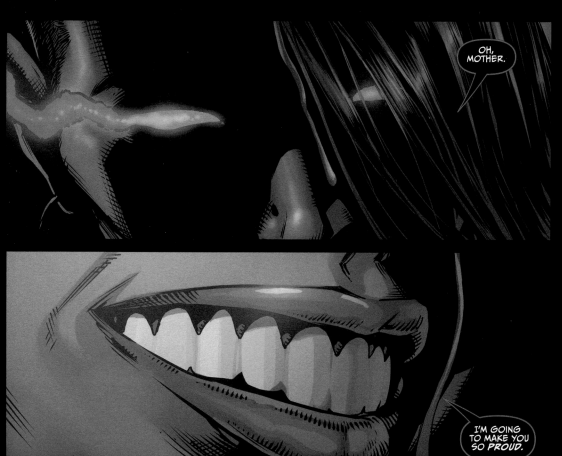

OH, MOTHER.

I'M GOING TO MAKE YOU SO *PROUD*.

THE WAR IS NOT OVER.

THE ANTI-LIFE HAS A *SECRET*. AND SOON I'LL SHARE THAT WITH THE WORLD.

YOU SACRIFICED SO MUCH FOR ME, MOTHER.

PING

"YOU LEFT THE ISLAND TO PROTECT ME.

I'M DOING THIS ALL FOR YOU.

PING

"THERE HE IS. THE FIRST MAN TO STEP FOOT ON THEMYSCIRA.

"STEVE TREVOR."

I NEED HIM.

THIS IS SUPERWOMAN'S CELL.

STAND BACK.

YES, YOU METALLIC MONSTER.

FREE HER.

HEY, CYBORG, MAYBE THIS ISN'T SUCH A GOOD IDEA--

SHE'S ONE OF *THREE* PEOPLE ON THE PLANET WHO MIGHT KNOW SOMETHING ABOUT THE ANTI-MONITOR. WHY HE'S HERE. HOW WE CAN STOP HIM.

I CAN'T ALWAYS CONTROL IT.

I TRY, BUT--

THE CRIME SYNDICATE'S WORLD WAS DESTROYED BY THE ANTI-MONITOR, POWER RING. IF ANYONE CAN GIVE US MORE INFORMATION ABOUT HIM, IT'S THEM.

THIS *RING* WAS WORN BY THE CRIME SYNDICATE'S TWISTED *GREEN LANTERN*, AND IT'S KIND OF *PSYCHED* WE'RE ABOUT TO *BREAK* INTO SUPERWOMAN'S CELL.

IT'S YOUR *ONLY* CHOICE, JESSICA.

I *REALLY* THINK WE SHOULD RECONSIDER. TRY AND LOCATE BATMAN AND GREEN LANTERN. THEY WERE SUPPOSED TO FIND OUT WHERE THE ANTI-MONITOR CAME FROM--

KNOWLEDGE AND EXPERIENCE ARE TWO DIFFERENT THINGS, JESSICA.

AND REALLY, YOU PATHETIC COW, YOU HAVE NEITHER WHEN IT COMES TO THIS RING.

QUIET--

...NOUGH OF THIS.

AAAHHH!!

NO MORE PRETENDING. NO MORE HIDING. NO MORE WAITING.

OUR PLAN GOES INTO ACTION NOW.

JESSICA?!

YOU TWO OKAY?

WE'RE OKAY.

FOR THE MOMENT.

YOU'RE WONDERING WHAT HAPPENED TO HIM. SUPERMAN'S ONLY STARTING TO REMEMBER HIMSELF.

HIS CELLS WERE DEPLETED WHEN HE AND LUTHOR WERE SENT TO APOKOLIPS, WHICH IS WHERE SUPERMAN LEFT LUTHOR...

...AFTER HE RECHARGED USING THE *SOLAR PITS*.

YOU SURE HE'S--

HE'S FINE, HAL.

SUPERMAN MAY HAVE HIS MENTAL CAPABILITIES BACK. HIS MIND MAY HAVE ADJUSTED TO THE ADDITIONAL *POWER* FLOWING THROUGH HIS BODY.

BUT IT'S TEMPORARY.

IS IT GOING TO WEAR OFF OR--

YOU'RE *FAR* FROM FINE.

THAT ENERGY IS BREAKING DOWN YOUR CELLULAR STRUCTURE.

"YOU'RE DYING, SUPERMAN."

THE EARTH IS CRACKING APART. THE ANTI-MONITOR IS HERE. HE KNOWS I'M TALKING ABOUT HIM. *HE'S COME FOR ME!*

HONEY, I TOLD YOU TO WAIT OUTSIDE. I WAS MAKING PROGRESS HERE.

THERE WAS A *GREEN EXPLOSION* DOWN THE HALL.

"SOMETHING'S WRONG WITH POWER RING."

MY DEAR SUPERWOMAN. IT'S TIME WE--

QUIET, POWER RING.

THE BABY'S TRYING TO SLEEP.

SUPERWOMAN--

HUSH LITTLE BABY, DON'T SAY A WORD. MAMA'S GONNA STEAL YOU A MOCKINGBIRD.

AND IF THAT MOCKINGBIRD DON'T SING, MAMA'S GONNA STEAL YOU A DIAMOND RING.

HANG TIGHT, JESS. I'VE CONNECTED WITH THAT RING BEFORE--

YOU CAN'T OVERRIDE MY RING.

IF YOU THINK I'M NOT GOING TO TRY--

--YOU'RE WRONG--

VICTOR STONE. CONNECTED.

DARKSEID WAR CHAPTER EIGHT: GODS OF JUSTICE PART TWO: CRIME PAYS

GEOFF JOHNS writer   **JASON FABOK** artist   **BRAD ANDERSON** colorist   **ROB LEIGH** letterer   **AMEDEO TURTURRO** assistant editor   **BRIAN CUNNINGHAM** group editor
cover by **JASON FABOK AND BRAD ANDERSON**

DESN'T SEEM TO BOTHER CLARK ANYMORE.

THE LEAGUE, HE'S CHANGED.

IT ALL BEGAN NEAR THE BEGINNING OF TIME ITSELF. WHEN A BEING NAMED MOBIUS CAME INTO CONTACT WITH THE **ANTI-LIFE EQUATION**.

IT **FUSED** WITH HIM, TRANSFORMING MOBIUS INTO THE **ANTI-MONITOR**.

LASHING OUT IN PAIN, HE BECAME A DESTROYER OF UNIVERSES.

OWLMAN TELLS US THE ANTI-MONITOR ANNIHILATED WORLD AFTER WORLD, INCLUDING THEIRS, UNTIL HE MET DARKSEID'S DAUGHTER, GRAIL.

GRAIL TOLD HIM THAT IF HE KILLED THE UNKILLABLE GOD OF APOKOLIPS, REALITY WOULD **FRACTURE** AND THE LINES BETWEEN **GODS** AND **MEN** WOULD BLUR. SOME BONDS WOULD **BREAK**, WHILE OTHERS WOULD **FORM**.

DURING THIS FRACTURE, THE ANTI-MONITOR WOULD BE ABLE TO **FREE** HIMSELF FROM THE ANTI-LIFE EQUATION.

IT ALL CAME TO PASS. AND THOUGH GRAIL HAS GONE MISSING WITH THE ANTI-LIFE EQUATION, MOBIUS IS ON EARTH SOMEWHERE, THREATENING TO DESTROY IT.

I SILENTLY PRAY TO THE GODS THAT I WILL FIND A WAY TO HELP FREE MY FRIENDS FROM THEIR NEW BURDENS AND STOP MOBIUS.

THE LEAGUE LOOK AT ME AS I PRAY. AS IF THEY CAN HEAR ME. AND THEY CAN. THEY LISTEN TO MY PRAYERS.

THAT'S WHAT GODS DO.

ARE WE SERIOUSLY HANDING OVER OUR *KRYPTONITE* TO ULTRAMAN? THIS STUFF'S LIKE *SUPER-CRACK* TO HIM.

AND I'M ALL FOR TAKING IT WHILE LEX IS OUT GETTING SOME "R&R" ON APOKOLIPS.

TECHNICALLY, IT ISN'T *OUR* KRYPTONITE, LANTERN. IT'S *LUTHOR'S.*

HELL, WE CAN STICK HIS *TOOTHBRUSH* DOWN OUR PANTS, TOO, IF YOU WANT.

JUST *TAKE* IT FROM THEM.

PATIENCE, ULTRAMAN.

ONE OF US IS GOING TO DIE.

DUDE! WHY WOULD YOU SAY THAT?

FLASH IS STILL HOST TO THE BLACK RACER, SHAZAM.

HE MAY HAVE THE ESSENCE OF DEATH UNDER CONTROL, BUT IT'S GOING TO *LEAK OUT* ON OCCASION.

DO YOU REALLY EXPECT US TO BELIEVE THAT IF WE GIVE YOU THE *KRYPTONITE,* YOU'LL HELP US SAVE *EARTH?*

WE DON'T CARE ABOUT YOUR *EARTH,* LANTERN.

MOBIUS DESTROYED *MY* GOTHAM.

AND *MY* METROPOLIS.

AND *MY* THEMYSCIRA.

YOU WANT TO *SAVE* YOUR PLANET.

WE WANT *REVENGE.*

IT'S THAT SIMPLE.

IT'S NOT SIMPLE AT ALL.

BEFORE WE AGREE TO ANYTHING, YOU'LL RELEASE *POWER RING* AND *CYBORG.*

JESSICA'S GONE, WONDER WOMAN. FOREVER BURIED DEEP IN THE RING WHILE I GET TO COME OUT AND PLAY.

AND YOUR CHANCES OF LOCATING AND DESTROYING THE ANTI-MONITOR WITHOUT US WILL BE DECREASED BY NINETY-EIGHT-POINT-THREE PERCENT.

THEY'RE OUR FRIENDS, NOT YOUR WEAPONS.

AFTER MOBIUS IS DEFEATED, WE'LL RETURN CYBORG AS LONG AS YOU PROVIDE A NEW BODY FOR GRID. ONE OF LEX LUTHOR'S ARMORED SUITS SHOULD DO.

BUT THE RING'S ALREADY *CHOSEN* JESSICA CRUZ, WONDER WOMAN, AND *NOTHING* CAN CHANGE THAT. NOT HER. NOT YOU. NOT ANYONE.

NOW DO YOU REALLY WANT TO CONTINUE TO ARGUE WITH US? I CAN ORDER GRID TO TELEPORT US HALFWAY ACROSS THIS EARTH. OR TO ANOTHER PLANET ENTIRELY.

YOU CAN WASTE YOUR TIME CHASING AFTER US WHILE MOBIUS DESTROYS YOUR PRECIOUS HOME.

WE DON'T CARE.

NEGOTIATIONS ARE OVER.

GIVE HIM THE KRYPTONITE.

YOU STEP OUT OF LINE, ULTRAMAN--

DON'T THREATEN ME, SUPERMAN. I'LL R-REMEMBER IT!

IT SMELLS SO G-GOOD.

LEXCORP SATELLITES ARE CAMOUFLAGED FROM CYBORG'S SYSTEM.

USE THE CODES LUTHOR PROVIDED ME.

THANK YOU, OWLMAN. CODES ACCEPTED. LINK ESTABLISHED. UPDATING SATELLITES. VIBRATIONAL SCANS ACTIVATED.

KRMMF

THIS IS ALL FOR YOU, MY CHILD.

CRIME SYNDICATE ASIDE, SHOULD WE REALLY BE TEAMING UP WITH A PREGNANT SUPER-VILLAIN?

YOU THINK SHE CANNOT FIGHT ON THE BATTLEFIELD? THAT NEVER STOPPED GRANNY GOODNESS.

I'M NEVER GOING TO GET THAT IMAGE OUT OF MY HEAD.

I KNOW OUR RINGS ARE DIFFERENT, BUT THERE HAS TO BE A WAY TO BREAK THROUGH TO JESSICA. IF I CAN JUST CONNECT MINE WITH HERS...

HAL, DO ME A FAVOR. KEEP ME IN SIGHT.

I MAY BE ABLE TO USE THE BLACK RACER AGAINST MOBIUS LIKE I DID DARKSEID. BUT I'M NOT SURE HOW MUCH LONGER I'LL BE ABLE TO CONTROL IT.

GRID HAS LOCATED MOBIUS.

GOOD.

I'M DONE EATING.

OTHAM CITY.

MY GOD! WHAT IS IT?

PLEASE! HELP ME! HELP--

DON'T STOP! DON'T LOOK BEHIND US!

TOMMY!

THAT ENERGY'S EATING *EVERYONE* IN ITS PATH.

PEOPLE NEED *HELP* OVER HERE!

CYBORG?!

OUR CONCERN IS FOR MOBIUS, SHAZAM, NOT FOR ANY OF THEM.

AHHH!

SO MANY OF THOSE SHADOWS. I'VE GOT TO ACCESS THESE *NEW GOD* POWERS.

DAMMIT, *WHY* DON'T I EVER GET AN *INSTRUCTION BOOK?* WHAT THE HECK WAS THAT *MARTIAN ONE?*

OH, RIGHT... *J'ONN'S WEAKNESS!*

COOL!

THE LEAGUE IS PROTECTING GOTHAM.

WHAT ABOUT THE SYNDICATE?

THEY'RE LOOKING FOR ME, WONDER WOMAN.

NOT THAT I DON'T WANT YOU TO FINALLY GET OFF YOUR ASS AND *DO* SOMETHING, BATS, BUT I'M GUESSING IF MOBIUS SITS IN HIS CHAIR WE'VE GOT *WORSE* PROBLEMS.

HAVE YOU NOTICED, LANTERN? THE SHADOWS AREN'T AFRAID OF YOUR LIGHT, BUT MINE...

LET ME OUT! THERE'S SOMEONE ELSE IN HERE WITH ME!

THEY FEAR IT!

I AM MORE THAN YOU *EVER* WILL BE!

MY RING MAY NOT BE FUELED BY *HATRED* LIKE YOURS, VOLTHOOM, BUT I'VE GOT SOMETHING *YOU* DON'T...

DARKSEID WAR SPECIAL: THE DARKNESS WITHIN

GEOFF JOHNS writer **IVAN REIS & JOE PRADO, OSCAR JIMENEZ, PAUL PELLETIER & TONY KORDOS** artists **ALEX SINCLAIR** colorist **ROB LEIGH** letterer
AMEDEO TURTURRO assistant editor **BRIAN CUNNINGHAM** group editor cover by **JASON FABOK AND BRAD ANDERSON**

THE NIGHT I WAS BORN, ZEUS CREATED A STORM THAT COVERED HALF THE GLOBE.

TO PROTECT THE ISLAND FROM HIS ENEMIES.

THE STORM WAS NOT FOR ME.

IT WAS FOR ZEUS' OWN DAUGHTER, DIANA.

HIPPOLYTA GAVE BIRTH TO HER IN THE JUNGLE...

...WHILE MY MOTHER GAVE BIRTH TO ME, HIGH IN THE FORBIDDEN MOUNTAINS.

THE SAME NIGHT, DIANA AND I. SYMMETRY BY DESIGN. FATE AT WORK. A TAPESTRY OF LIVES WOVEN TOGETHER THAT ONLY THE GODS CAN SEE. THE ORACLE HAS FORETOLD IT-- OUR LIVES WILL BE FOREVER CONNECTED.

IF HIPPOLYTA AND THE OTHERS HAD KNOWN OF MY BIRTH, THEY WOULD HAVE SLAUGHTERED ME THEN AND THERE.

MOTHER WAS FORCED TO ABANDON HER LIFE ON THEMYSCIRA TO PROTECT ME.

YOUR DAUGHTER IS BEAUTIFUL, MY QUEEN.

MERCY.

ALTHOUGH MOTHER WAS
THE GREATEST ASSASSIN THE
AMAZONS HAD EVER KNOWN,
SHE SPARED THEIR LIVES.

GRAIL?!

MOTHER, I...

...I'M SCARED.

SHE NEVER HIT ME. SHE NEVER YELLED. SHE ONLY HELD ME CLOSE.

AM I EVIL?

NO, MY CHILD.

THINGS WERE NEVER QUITE THE SAME AFTER THAT.

THE NEXT DAY, WE TRAVELED TO ROME, TO A SECRET CAVERN UNDER THE SEVEN HILLS.

COUNTLESS TIMES I MADE MOTHER TELL ME THE TALE OF HOW SHE ONCE BEAT THE GRIFFIN. SHE HAD SPARED ITS LIFE AND IN RETURN IT OFFERED HER ITS ETERNAL SERVITUDE.

SHE'D COME TO COLLECT ON THAT PROMISE.

IT WOULD BE A GREAT ALLY FOR US, MOTHER SAID.

THE GRIFFIN WATCHED OVER HER EVERY NIGHT.

PROTECTING HER.

FROM EVERYONE.

FOR DECADES WE REMAINED HIDDEN AS MY TRAINING CONTINUED, MOTHER OFTEN LEAVING TO INTERCEDE IN MEN'S WARS.

SHE MADE MANY ENEMIES.

AND SOME FRIENDS.

WHENEVER SHE ATTEMPTED TO RECRUIT THESE NEW FRIENDS TO HELP US, I WOULD LOSE CONTROL.

AND SOON IT WOULD BE ONLY THE TWO OF US AGAIN.

ALTHOUGH SHE WEPT, SHE KNEW IT WAS FOR THE BEST.

THE HUMANS WERE MORTAL ANYWAY, BUT SHE AND I...

WE ARE FOREVER, MOTHER.

THEN THERE CAME THE DAY OUR PLAN TO DESTROY DARKSEID BEGAN. MOTHER HAD LOCATED THE LAST OF THE THREE BLIND WITCHES.

SHE HAD THE EYE OF SEEING.

DESPITE MOTHER'S PROTESTS, THERE WAS NO TIME TO DELAY. I SLAYED THE LAST OF THE WITCHES AND TOOK IT.

WITH THE EYE, I SAW THE BEING WHO HAD THE POWER TO DESTROY MY FATHER. THE ANTI-MONITOR.

I SOUGHT HIM OUT, TRAVELING ACROSS THE MULTIVERSE. I TOLD HIM HOW HE COULD BECOME FREE FROM THE ANTI-LIFE. BY KILLING MY FATHER, THE BONDS BETWEEN THE GODS AND MORTALS WOULD BREAK MOMENTARILY.

AND SO WE DID JUST THAT.

"I'M WORRIED ABOUT YOU, GRAIL."

DARKSEID WAR CHAPTER NINE: POWER MAD

GEOFF JOHNS writer JASON FABOK artist BRAD ANDERSON colorist ROB LEIGH letterer AMEDEO TURTURRO assistant editor BRIAN CUNNINGHAM group editor
cover by JASON FABOK AND BRAD ANDERSON

WASN'T I CLEAR, WONDER WOMAN? GET AWAY FROM--

SHE'S ABOUT TO GIVE *BIRTH.* WE NEED TO GET SUPERWOMAN SOMEWHERE SAFE. AWAY FROM MOBIUS.

AWAY FROM HIM?

WE'RE NOT GOING *ANYWHERE.* THAT'S THE ENTIRE *POINT.*

SUPERWOMAN SCREAMS AND EVERY PIECE OF GLASS IN GOTHAM SHATTERS. THE EARTH CRACKS BENEATH US. AND OWLMAN WAITS...

AAAHHHH!

...WHILE MOBIUS FIGHTS HIS WAY TOWARDS BATMAN. HE WANTS THE CHAIR BACK. WE DON'T KNOW WHY.

STAND ASIDE, LEX LUTHOR, AND I WILL BURN YOU FROM EXISTENCE QUICKLY. YOU CANNOT PROTECT THE LEAGUE FROM ME FOR LONG. MY SHADOW DEMONS--

ARE BURNIN... AWAY. CONSUM... BY THE OMEG... EFFECT. BUT ... ARMY...

THE PARADEMONS?

THEY DIE.

THEN I'LL OBLIGE.

BUT THEY DO NOT FEAR IT. NO PAIN. NO EMOTION. LIKE KILLING UNIVERSES FROM AFAR, IT IS UTTERLY UNSATISFYING.

I THIRST FOR SUFFERING.

THOSE THAT STARTED THIS WAR...THEY CLAIMED TO BE DOING IT IN THE NAME OF THE MISSION OF THE AMAZONS.

BUT YOU DON'T START A WAR TO ... AND END A WAR ...

VIOLENCE BEGETS VIOLENCE.

UNLESS SOMEONE BREAKS THE CYCLE.

THAT'S USUALLY ME.

YOU TOLD US THAT THERE WAS A WAY TO STOP MOBIUS. THAT YOU WOULD TELL US WHEN IT WAS TIME. I'D SAY THIS QUALIFIES.

YES. WE HAVE A WEAPON THAT CAN KILL HIM.

WHAT WEAPON?

I KNOW.

THE CHAIR KNOWS, DIANA.

THAT'S WHY MOBIUS WANTS IT. HE WANTS TO LEARN THE SECRET TO THIS "WEAPON" OWLMAN'S REFERRING TO.

PING

THE BABY.

SO YOU KNOW. THAT'S FINE. ONCE THE CHILD IS BORN, WE'LL TAKE CARE OF MOBIUS AND THEN YOU.

HURRY UP AND GET IT OUT ALREADY, SUPERWOMAN. WE DON'T HAVE ALL DAY.

THE JUSTICE LEAGUE WILL KEEP MOBIUS BUSY, VOLTHOOM. AS THEY FALL ONE BY ONE.

I HOPE NOT ALL OF THEM. I'D LIKE TO PICK ONE OR TWO APART MYSELF.

I STOLE THIS DISC FROM MANTIS. HE STOLE IT FROM LIGHTRAY. IT SHOULD DISPERSE THE SHADOWS.

WHY WOULD WE HELP HIM?

THIS HUMAN HAS THE POWER OF DARKSEID FLOWING THROUGH HIS VEINS NOW, SCOT.

BUT LEX LUTHOR IS ON OUR SIDE, BARDA.

"HE'S WORKING WITH SUPERMAN, BATMAN AND WONDER WOMAN. HE WANTS TO SAVE THIS WORLD AS MUCH AS WE DO."

WE NEED TO PRIORITIZE. THE SYNDICATE--

THEY'RE ONLY CONCERNED ABOUT SUPERWOMAN. MOBIUS IS THE MORE DANGEROUS THREAT NOW.

WHY CALL THE BABY A WEAPON?

BECAUSE OF ITS FATHER.

AND WHO IS THAT?

PING

SCOT, DARKSEID IS DEAD. THE PARADEMONS ARE HERE, AWAY FROM APOKOLIPS.

FOR THE FIRST TIME IN OUR LIFETIMES, OUR HOME IS LEFT UNGUARDED.

IF WE RETURN NOW, WE COULD BREAK OPEN THE SLAVE CAMPS. WE COULD LEAD THE GREATEST *REVOLT* APOKOLIPS HAS EVER SEEN!

THIS MAY BE OUR ONLY CHANCE TO *FREE* APOKOLIPS, SCOT.

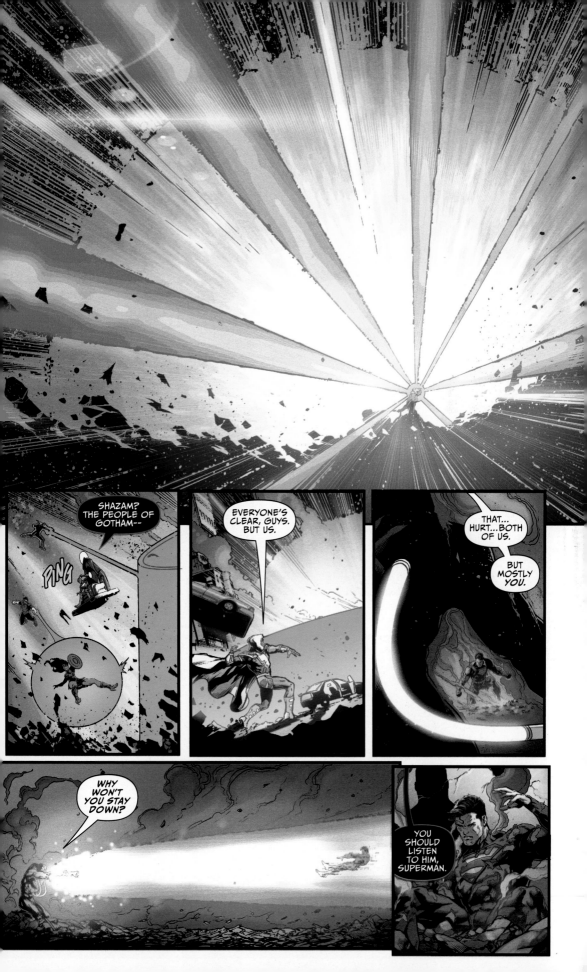

ALL THIS TIME, I'VE WONDERED ABOUT YOU. WHETHER YOU'VE HELD YOUR POWER BACK OR NOT. FEELING POWER MYSELF, I BELIEVE YOU HAVE. BUT WHY? BECAUSE YOU DIDN'T WANT TO HURT ANYONE? OR CROSS AN IMAGINARY ETHICAL OR POLITICAL LINE?

OR ARE YOU *AFRAID* OF IT?

YOU'RE PROJECTING AS USUAL, LEX.

MAYBE SO. MAYBE NOT.

YOU SHOULD BE AFR-FRAID...

WHAT IS IT, FLASH?

...I'M T-TRYING TO HELP BUT... IT'S MAKING ME WAIT.

GOD, IT HURTS TO STAND STILL AND WAIT.

WAIT FOR WHAT?

DEATH IS COMING.

HEIR TO DARKSEID.

YOU WILL SUFFER HIS FATE.

LOOK INTO MY EYES AND SHOW ME. SHOW ME HOW MUCH IT HURTS.

WHISPER YOUR REGRETS.

PRAY.

SCREAM.

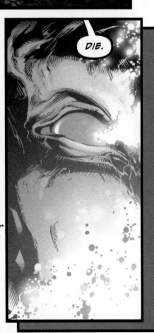

DIE.

I'LL SAY IT IS.

BY THE GODS.

PING PING PING PING PING PING PING PING

NNN.

"STEVE?"

YET *ANOTHER* HUMAN INFUSED WITH THE POWER OF A GOD. HE WILL DIE WITH THE OTHERS.

STEVE--!!

GRAIL, WHAT ARE YOU DOING?

HAVING FUN!

DO IT, TREVOR.

D-DIANA... HELP ME.

GEOFF JOHNS writer   JASON FABOK artist   BRAD ANDERSON colorist   ROB LEIGH letterer   AMEDEO TURTURRO assistant editor   BRIAN CUNNINGHAM group editor
cover by JASON FABOK AND BRAD ANDERSON

HER NAME IS GRAIL.

SHE IS THE DAUGHTER OF AN AMAZON AND OF DARKSEID, BORN ON THE HIDDEN ISLAND OF THEMYSCIRA THE SAME NIGHT I WAS.

HER MOTHER, MYRINA, TOOK GRAIL AND ESCAPED THE ISLAND, RAISING HER IN SECRET WITH ONE PURPOSE: TO DESTROY HER FATHER.

GRAIL TRAVELED ACROSS THE MULTIVERSE IN SEARCH OF SOMEONE CAPABLE AND WILLING TO GO TO WAR WITH DARKSEID.

SHE FOUND A BEING FUSED WITH THE ANTI-LIFE EQUATION--

--THE ONE THING THAT DARKSEID WAS VULNERABLE TO.

AND SO GRAIL AND MYRINA ORCHESTRATED A WAR BETWEEN THE ANTI-MONITOR AND DARKSEID. HERE. ON EARTH.

DARKSEID WAS ANNIHILATED AND THE ANTI-MONITOR WAS FREED FROM THE ANTI-LIFE EQUATION.

IN THE WAKE OF DARKSEID'S DESTRUCTION, REALITY RUPTURED. POWER CHANGED HANDS. WHILE GRAIL TOOK THE ANTI-LIFE FOR HERSELF, MY FRIENDS--THE JUSTICE LEAGUE-- BECAME GODS.

LEX LUTHOR
GOD OF APOKOLIPS

SHAZAM
GOD OF GODS

BATMAN
GOD OF KNOWLEDGE

THE FLASH
GOD OF DEATH

SUPERMAN
GOD OF STRENGTH

I BELIEVED WE WOULD STOP THE ANTI-MONITOR.

UNTIL GRAIL CREATED HER OWN NEW GOD AND DESTROYED HIM HERSELF.

DO YOU, BATMAN?

LIKE FATHER, LIKE DAUGHTER.

PING

PING

YOU ACCOMPLISHED YOUR MISSION. YOUR FATHER IS DEAD. BUT THE MOBIUS CHAIR SAYS THAT EVEN THOUGH YOU'VE FULFILLED YOUR "PURPOSE," YOU'VE BECOME INTOXICATED WITH POWER.

YOU WANT MORE.

I GOT HER--

YOU'RE RIGHT, BATMAN. I'VE DONE MY TASK.

AND NOW FOR ANOTHER.

THE DESTRUCTION OF THE JUSTICE LEAGUE.

STARTING WITH YOU, SLAVE OF APOKOLIPS.

WHAT HAPPENED TO THE OLD EARTH SAYING, "THE ENEMY OF MY ENEMY IS MY FRIEND"?

YOU WON'T ESCAPE--

"YOU WON'T ESCAPE ME"? OR "YOU WON'T ESCAPE THIS TIME"? I'VE HEARD THEM ALL BEFORE, GRAIL. THINK OF SOMETHING MORE ORIGINAL.

CHAINS WON'T HOLD ME.

THAT'D BE OUR GUESS, TOO.

LANTERNS.

A WHOLE CORPS OF THEM, LADY.

JOHN AND I USUALLY PLAY THE GOOD-COP/BAD-COP ROUTINE, BUT WHO AM I KIDDING? COMPARED TO YOU, WE'RE ONLY GONNA COME OUT LOOKING GOOD.

MY AX WAS FORGED BY HADES HIMSELF.

IT CAN SLICE THROUGH A GOD.

I WILL NOT BE CAGED.

MY RING IS CHARGED. I'M READY TO LEAVE THIS WORLD.

AS AM--

YOU'RE NOT GOING ANYWHERE UNTIL YOU LET MY FRIENDS GO!

I HAVE THE POWER OF *EVERY GOD* AT MY FINGERTIPS AND I'LL--

MAZAHS!!

AAARGHH!

THIS WORLD IS A LOST CAUSE.

YOU ARE AFRAID, VOLTHOOM--

NEVER. WHERE THE HELL DID OWLMAN GO?

THE GREEN REALM OF THE POWER RING.

THE BLACK RACER IS GAINING ON FLASH.

WE NEED TO HELP HIM, VIC.

WHATEVER YOUR PLAN WAS TO PUT ME BACK IN THE DRIVER'S SEAT--

SHAZAM'S DISTRACTED THEM. GIVEN ME A FOOTHOLD TO HACK INTO. I'M TRYING TO TAP INTO THE RING'S SUPERNATURAL TECHNOLOGY. SEE IF I CAN OVERRIDE VOLTHOOM'S CONTROL OF YOUR BODY--

--BUT THE PROGRAMMING...IT'S NOT ONLY *ONES* AND *ZEROES* I'M SORTING THROUGH. THERE'S A *THIRD* NUMERICAL QUANTITY. A NUMBER THAT ONLY EXISTS INSIDE VOLTHOOM'S RING.

I CAN ONLY DESCRIBE IT AS...FEAR.

NO ROOM FOR FEAR RIGHT NOW.

"THIS WEIRD *FEAR NUMBER* THAT'S GRINDING UP THE GEARS..."

...I THINK YOU'RE HELPING ME *BYPASS* IT SOMEHOW. WHATEVER YOU'RE FEELING, JESS, KEEP IT UP.

YEAH. I CAN *READ* THE TECH. I CAN GET YOU BACK *IN*...BUT ONLY MOMENTARILY.

YOU'LL HAVE *ONE SECOND* BEFORE VOLTHOOM TAKES BACK CONTROL.

ONE SECOND IS ALL I NEED.

BARRY IS GOING TO DIE.

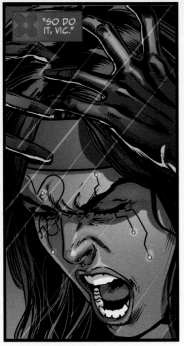

"SO DO IT, VIC."

DAD. IRIS.

BARRY?!

WHO WAS--?

"SEND ME BACK NOW!"

SHE'S GONE...

AS IS THE OMEGA EFFECT. THE WITCH STOLE MY POWER WITH THAT CHILD--

SHOW SOME RESPECT AND SHUT YOUR MOUTH, LUTHOR.

WHY? BECAUSE THE *GREEN-LANTERN-WHO-WASN'T* IS DEAD? SHE BETRAYED US ANYWAY.

IT WASN'T JESSICA WHO BETRAYED US, LEX. IT WAS THAT DAMN RING.

JESSICA DIED SAVING THE FLASH'S LIFE.

WE NEED TO PUT AN *END* TO ALL OF THIS.

AN *END*?

OH, IT *WILL* END, DIANA. BUT IT WILL END *MY* WAY.

I AM *GRAIL* THE *GODKILLER*.

AND TODAY *ALL* OF YOUR GODS *DIE*.

GODS?

WE FAIL.

PING
PING
PING
AAAHHHH!!!
PING

OH, YES. THE CURSE OF METRON IS NOT SOMETHING I WANT.

WHAT IS IT YOU HUMANS SAY?

TOO MUCH INFORMATION.

BUT BATMAN *HAS* TOLD ME SOMETHING I NEEDED TO KNOW. STEVE TREVOR IS NOT THE *CHOSEN ONE*.

MAZAHS!

SO LET ME TAKE THE *ANTI-LIFE EQUATION* BACK.

PING PING
PING NG
NG RNG
PING
RNG RNG

SO THAT THERE CAN BE A *NEW* BIRTH.

BUT THE BEST OF US NEVER GIVE UP.

THE MOBIUS CHAIR IS *MINE* NOW.

PING

RELEASE CYBORG, GRID. JOIN THE CHAIR. WE'RE LEAVING.

YES, OWLMAN. DOWNLOADING...

...DOWNLOADED.

IT'S TIME FOR PLAN "B."

PING

HAVE A NICE DAY.

BOOM

IN A BURST OF LIGHT, THE LAST OF THE SYNDICATE VANISH. CYBORG STUMBLES, REBOOTS--THEN REJOINS THE LEAGUE--

--AND THE ARMY OF APOKOLIPS.

WE FIGHT TOGETHER.

BUT NOTHING SLOWS THEM DOWN.

DIANA?

THERE'S NO MORE REASON TO FIGHT, GRAIL.

YOU ARE AN AMAZON. YOU ARE MY SISTER. WE CAN--

I AM NO ONE'S SISTER!

KRREEE

DIANA, THE CHAIR...IT TOLD ME THE ANTI-LIFE EQUATION HAS THE POWER TO CONTROL *EVERY* LIVING BEING IN THE UNIVERSE--OR IT HAS THE POWER TO CONTROL *DARKSEID.*

WE HAVE TO SEPARATE IT FROM DARKSEID. THE POWER WITHIN WILL BE DISPERSED. IT WILL ALL SHUT DOWN.

BUT ONLY *GRAIL* CAN REVERSE WHAT SHE'S DONE.

YOU SEEK THE *TRUTH* WITH THE LASSO? IS THAT WHAT YOU BOTH *WANT?*

THE TRUTH IS YOU *ARE* AN AMAZON. AND YOU CAN DO THE *RIGHT* THING.

IT'S NOT TOO LATE, GRAIL.

IT *IS!* IT'S TOO LATE FOR ME.

I AM DARKNESS. I AM EVIL!

"HE HAS RETURNED."

YES, ARDORA. I'VE COME BACK TO APOKOLIPS.

FOR A REVOLUTION.

ALL SWEAR LOYALTY TO THE GREAT HERO OF METROPOLIS!

"THE POWER YOU GAINED ON APOKOLIPS CHANGED YOU, SUPERMAN."

EXACTLY HOW, DR. STONE?

DARKSEID IS GONE. APOKOLIPS IS READY.

WE'VE FORGED YOUR SYMBOL FOR YOU. THE FIGHT BEGINS.

YES. MY SYMBOL.

"BATMAN WAS CORRECT."

YOU'RE DYING.

I HAVE TO ADMIT...

PING PING PING PING

LEX

"LEX!"

KLK

BRUCE?

WANTED TO MAKE SURE YOU'RE OKAY.

I'M FINE.

THOUGH I WAS WRONG.

ABOUT WHAT?

THE RING ISN'T THE HERO.

FORGET ABOUT THAT...

METRON HAS BEEN A MOST HELPFUL ALLY.

I APPRECIATE THE FREEDOM, OWLMAN, AND NOW THAT I'VE TAUGHT YOU HOW TO ACCESS THE MOBIUS CHAIR PROPERLY, I PRESUME WE'RE FINISHED HERE.

I ADVISE YOU NOT TO TRUST HIM, OWLMAN.

YOU'RE WRONG, GRID.

BUT A WARNING: DO NOT SEEK TOO MANY ANSWERS. YOUR MIND--

PING IS STRONGER THAN BATMAN'S. I CAN PROCESS IT ALL.

SO TELL ME EVERYTHING, CHAIR. TELL ME ALL THE SECRETS OF THE UNI--

PING PING PING

NO.

WHAT IS IT?

HE'S HERE. HE'S--

JUSTICE LEAGUE #47
HARLEY'S LITTLE BLACK BOOK VARIANT BY JIM LEE,
SCOTT WILLIAMS & ALEX SINCLAIR

JUSTICE LEAGUE #48
ADULT COLORING VARIANT BY SCOTT KOLINS

WONDER WOMAN #49, SUPERMAN/WONDER WOMAN #26 AND
JUSTICE LEAGUE: DARKSEID WAR SPECIAL #1
VARIANT TRIPTYCH BY KIM JUNG GI

JUSTICE LEAGUE #49
BATMAN V SUPERMAN VARIANT BY MATTEO SCALERA & MORENO DINISIO

JUSTICE LEAGUE #50
VARIANT BY JOHN ROMITA JR., SCOTT HANNA & ALEX SINCLAIR